OFFICIAL UNIVERSAL STUDIOS MONSTERS

PRESENTS

Dracula™

Adapted from the Universal film *Dracula*
by Mike Teitelbaum

Illustrated by Art Ruiz

Western Publishing Company, Inc., Racine, Wisconsin 53404

Official Universal Studios Monsters™ & © 1992 Universal City Studios, Inc. All rights reserved. Licensed by MCA/Universal Merchandising, Inc. Printed in the U.S.A. No part of this book may be reproduced or copied in any form without written permission from the copyright owner. All other trademarks are the property of Western Publishing Company, Inc. Library of Congress Catalog Card Number: 91-78364 ISBN: 0-307-22331-0
A MCMXCII

To Bela, for bringing the vampire to "life"
and
To S.S., for the opportunity to "Achieve Creepy"
—M.T.

Contents

CHAPTER 1
Arrival in Transylvania

The sun was beginning to set behind the eerie Transylvanian mountains. Two rocky cliffs were silhouetted against the early evening sky. An old dirt road wound through them, forming a narrow mountain pass.

As the sun sank lower, a large weatherbeaten stagecoach carrying five passengers sped along the bumpy road. Four galloping horses furiously pulled the coach at top speed. The driver leaned forward in his seat, gripping the reins tightly, and shouted at the horses: "On with you! Faster!"

He was in a hurry to reach his destination before dark. He had heard many stories about Transylvania from local villagers, who whispered about dangers that lurked there in the night.

Inside the stagecoach the passengers were being

1

jostled back and forth by the rough ride. A very proper Englishwoman, on a tour of the area, sat grasping her carpetbag. Her secretary, a small, worried-looking woman, turned the pages of a book on Transylvanian culture and customs. She had just read aloud from it to the Englishwoman, an experienced world traveler and a person not easily frightened by local legends and superstitions. The secretary, however, was terrified by what she had read.

A Transylvanian couple sitting across from the Englishwoman and her secretary glanced out the window at the setting sun, then looked at each other nervously. They, too, knew the horrible stories about the evil that lurked in the countryside. Although the couple were on their way home, they planned to spend the night at the inn where the coach would soon stop. The man took his wife's hand into his own and squeezed it reassuringly, trying to convince himself as much as her that everything would be all right, that they would reach the inn and be safely indoors before the sun had fully set.

The fifth passenger was a young English lawyer named Renfield. Unlike the other passengers, he was here on business. He carried a briefcase full of important documents for his Transylvanian client to sign.

Renfield still had a long night of travel ahead of him, for he was going to remain on the coach after it let the other passengers out at the inn. He planned to travel up into the mountains, where he was supposed to meet a carriage that would bring him to the castle of his client.

"Where were we in our reading, Sara?" asked the Englishwoman.

Her secretary found the place in the book and began to read aloud: "'Transylvania is one of the wildest and least-known parts of Central Europe. Among the rugged peaks that frown down upon Borgo Pass are the crumbling castles of an age long gone.'"

"Borgo Pass?" repeated Renfield. "Why, that's where I'm headed tonight."

The local couple looked at him, then shook their heads.

"Is something wrong?" the young man asked.

Before anyone could answer, the stagecoach increased its speed and lurched forward, slamming Renfield back into his seat. He stuck his head out the window. "I say!" he shouted at the driver. "A bit slower up there!"

The local couple exchanged frightened glances. Then the husband grabbed Renfield by the arm. "No!" he cried excitedly. "Don't ask him to slow down. We must reach the inn before sunset!"

"But why?"

"The nights here in Transylvania are evil," the

local man explained. "After sunset the undead leave their graves and feast on the blood of the living!"

Renfield raised his eyebrows and glanced toward the Englishwoman, who was sneering.

"If you lived in these parts, you would not sneer, madam!" the local man said sharply.

The passengers grew quiet as the stagecoach rolled on toward its destination.

Soon it clattered through the large iron gates of the inn's courtyard. Renfield noticed a strange-looking herb hanging above each of the inn's many windows. Then, as the horses came to a noisy halt, he saw the same herb hanging above the front door. "What on earth is that bizarre-looking herb that's hanging everywhere?" he wondered aloud.

"Wolfsbane!" replied the local man. "It protects us from the vampires!"

Renfield shook his head in disbelief.

The inn was a low building made of stone. Its sloping thatched roof showed signs of age, for the inn had stood there for nearly one hundred years.

The passengers got out of the coach and waited while the driver tossed their luggage from the top of the vehicle to the inn's porter, standing below.

"Driver, please don't take my luggage down," called Renfield. "I'm going on to Borgo Pass tonight."

The driver glanced at Renfield. Then, ignoring

these words, he started to toss the lawyer's bags down as well.

"No, no, I say!" shouted Renfield, annoyed. "Please put that bag back up there!"

The innkeeper, hearing Renfield's shouts, rushed out of the inn and ran over to the stagecoach. He apologized to the young Englishman, then spoke with the driver in his native language.

"The driver is afraid," said the innkeeper. "There is evil in the Transylvanian night. He says you should spend the night here and go on after sunrise."

"I'm terribly sorry," said Renfield. "But there's a carriage meeting me this evening at Borgo Pass."

The innkeeper looked at him strangely. "Borgo Pass?" he repeated.

Renfield nodded.

"And whose carriage is meeting you?" the innkeeper asked suspiciously.

"Count Dracula's," the other replied.

Hearing this name, the local couple gasped in horror, and the innkeeper stared in disbelief at Renfield. "Count Dracula?" he cried. "You are going to Castle Dracula?"

"Yes, that's right," said Renfield, puzzled by their reaction. "Count Dracula has hired my professional services."

"No!" shouted the innkeeper. "You must not go

there! There are vampires at that castle! Dracula and his wives leave their coffins at night and drink the blood of the living!"

The Englishwoman, who had been standing nearby, let out a sigh of impatience. "Rubbish!" she snapped. "I've never heard such absolute nonsense in my life!" She turned and headed toward the inn's front door, her secretary scurrying along after her.

"Look," said the innkeeper, pointing at the mountains. "The sun has almost set. When it is gone, they will leave their coffins. Come! We must all go inside."

"But this is just superstition," Renfield protested. "There's nothing to be afraid of. Please tell the driver that I'm here on a very important business matter, and that I've really got to go on."

The innkeeper shrugged and turned to his wife, who had joined them outside. She looked at her husband, then removed a small cross on a black ribbon that was hanging around her neck. Clasping it in her hand, she walked toward Renfield, who was about to get into the stagecoach. "Wait!" she shouted, stepping up to the coach. "Please, wait."

Renfield, slightly annoyed at yet another delay, looked at her.

"If you really must go tonight," the innkeeper's wife continued, "wear this." She held up the cross. "It will protect you!"

The young lawyer looked at the cross and hesitated. If I humor her, he thought, I still might be able to keep my appointment. "Very well," he said. "I'll take it."

The innkeeper's wife kissed the cross, then gently placed it around Renfield's neck.

"Thank you," he said as he reboarded the coach. Then he cried, "Driver, let's be off! And hurry, please!"

The driver cracked the reins, and the horses sprang into a gallop, pulling the coach out past the inn's gates toward the eerie mountains.

When the stagecoach had disappeared from view, the innkeeper locked the gates securely and everyone hurried inside. Soon the last rays of the sun disappeared behind the mountains.

Castle Dracula was perched high on top of a mountain peak. This ancient castle had for many centuries been the home of Transylvanian royalty. Aristocrats from many lands had been its guests, sharing in the joyous celebrations and magnificent ceremonies that had taken place within its walls. But that was all in the past. This once-magnificent structure was now in ruins.

The moon had risen in the night sky and now cast an unearthly glow on the castle walls. Pieces of broken stone lay on the ground. Once-lush gardens were overgrown with weeds. Iron gates were rusted, and windows that had been shattered decades before remained open to the elements. But the castle's current owner, the infamous Count Dracula, had no need for a luxurious home. This decaying building was perfect for his needs.

Deep in the cellar of the castle was a series of connecting rooms and hallways. In the twisting, turning passageways were old burial crypts, the final resting places for generations of Transylvanian royalty.

In one lofty crypt, with tiny windows set up high, filthy water trickled down the stone walls, now mildewed after years of decay. The air was thick with the disgusting stench of death.

Large bugs busily crawled in and out of the cracks that split the crypt's walls and floors. Packs of squealing rats scurried around the room, stopping here and there to gnaw on the bones of rotting corpses.

A glimmer of moonlight shot through one of the small, high windows and fell upon a coffin. Slowly its lid began to rise. Long, bony fingers emerged from within, grasping the lid and pushing it open.

Count Dracula sat up in his coffin. The sun had set on another day. It was nighttime, the time when he came alive. Suddenly wolves began to howl outside.

Dracula stepped from his coffin and closed it. He raised himself up to his full height. He was a tall man, with bloodless, chalk-white skin pulled tightly against his fine-boned face. His straight jet-black hair formed a perfect V over his forehead.

He was dressed formally in black tuxedo pants and a gray vest, with a stiff white shirt and a small bow tie. A magnificent black opera cape hung from his shoulders.

Count Dracula turned to three other coffins lying in the crypt, raised his hand, and extended his long fingers. The lids slowly opened, and from each coffin emerged a beautiful chalk-white woman. They were Dracula's wives, women whose blood he had fed upon during their lives. When they died, he commanded them to walk the earth at night; he was able to control their bodies and their minds. Now they were like Dracula himself—one of the undead—vampires who fed upon the blood of the living.

Dracula stared at his wives with burning red eyes, silently ordering them to leave the castle, to hunt for victims in the darkness outside. The women moved as if in a trance, climbing the dark stone stairs, then walking out into the eerie Transylvanian night.

Dracula slowly drew his cape around himself and also headed for the stairs. He had an appointment to keep, and it was time to meet his visitor.

Outside, in the distance, the wolves howled again.

CHAPTER 2

Journey to Castle Dracula

The stagecoach carrying Renfield sped along the road leading to Borgo Pass, its horses straining at their bits as the coach's wheels rolled over the surface.

Looking out the window, the young Englishman saw huge, weirdly shaped rocks and strange-looking trees with twisted black limbs. Dark clouds drifted across the moonlit sky as a thick mist closed in around the mountains. The rising mist and streaming moonlight cast an eerie spell over the bleak landscape, sending a chill down Renfield's spine.

He remembered the innkeeper's warning and the frightened looks the local folk had given him as he left the inn. Although he didn't believe their superstitious nonsense, he was looking forward to being safe within the walls of Castle Dracula.

When the stagecoach came to an old wooden sign that read BORGO PASS, the driver pulled hard on his reins, bringing the coach to a squeaking halt. Suddenly his horses reared up on their hind legs and whinnied in fear, terrified by the sight of a long black carriage that stood nearby. The driver pulled hard on his reins once more, calming his horses down.

As soon as Renfield stepped out of the coach, the driver threw his bags on the ground, grabbed the reins, and urged the horses to move. The coach took off at a mad gallop, leaving Renfield behind in the dark, chilly Transylvanian night. He picked up his bags and walked over to the waiting carriage.

Count Dracula himself was standing beside the carriage, although he didn't reveal his identity to Renfield, who thought he was the driver. His huge cape covered his face, so that only his red eyes were visible. As Renfield approached him, Dracula stared at the Englishman but said nothing.

"Is this the carriage from Count Dracula?" Renfield asked nervously.

Dracula nodded. Then, taking Renfield's bags, he gestured for his visitor to get into the carriage. The door swung open, seemingly under its own power. Renfield was puzzled, but he stepped into the vehicle and closed the door.

Dracula climbed into the driver's seat, then

snapped the reins. The carriage lunged forward, the horses' hooves loudly pounding on the dirt road.

Inside, the young lawyer, thrown from side to side, tried to brace himself against his seat. As the carriage went along, however, the ride grew bumpier. Finally Renfield stuck his head out the window. "Driver," he yelled, "could you slow down a—" He stopped short and stared, stunned by what he saw.

The driver's seat was empty, and the reins hung limply over the front of the carriage. A huge bat flew above the horses' heads, its giant wings flapping rhythmically as it kept up with the horses.

Shocked, Renfield pulled his head back inside and sank into his seat. Where could the driver have gone? he wondered. And who was controlling the carriage?

Outside, a lone wolf howled. A second wolf answered the first, followed by another, then another. Renfield, terrified, gripped his seat for the rest of the journey.

Soon Castle Dracula was in sight. Renfield glanced out at the ancient structure, a crumbling ruin sharply silhouetted against the night sky. Was this really the home of his wealthy client? he wondered.

The carriage moved past the large oak gates and came to a stop in front of the main door. Here the castle's decay was even more noticeable. A decrepit fountain stood in the center of the overgrown courtyard. It seemed as if no one had been here for centuries.

Renfield stepped out of the carriage and walked around to the driver's seat. It was still empty. Somehow the horses had found their way to the castle on their own. The Englishman searched for his bags, but they were gone.

Nearby, the wolves resumed their howling.

Renfield, frightened, walked up to the castle's front door, which swung open on its own. Seeing no one, he cautiously stepped inside.

The main hallway was very long, completely empty, and dark save for thin shafts of moonlight streaming in through holes in the broken walls. Dust and cobwebs were everywhere, and pieces of plaster were strewn about on the damp stone floor. Several bats fluttered down from the high ceiling, swooping past Renfield and flying out the open front door. Then the door closed behind them.

In the rear of the hallway stood a large winding staircase that led to the upper levels of the castle. Halfway up, above the first landing, a huge spiderweb completely covered the staircase. In front of this web stood Count Dracula.

He was still dressed in formal clothes and carried

a large flickering candle that sent light dancing on the castle walls. As he came down the stairs toward Renfield, his black cape billowed behind him.

"I am Dracula," he said when he reached the bottom of the stairs, bowing and smiling at Renfield.

Renfield, surprised by the appearance of his host and by the ruined state of the castle, hesitated for a moment, his mouth gaping open. "It's a relief to meet you," he finally replied nervously. "I don't know what happened to the driver or to my luggage." He looked around, then back at Dracula. "With the castle in this state of disrepair, I honestly thought I was in the wrong place."

"The walls of my castle are broken," began Dracula, "and the shadows are many. But I bid you welcome. Come with me."

Renfield followed the Count up the stairs. When they reached the first landing, the wolves resumed howling outside, and Dracula stopped. "Listen to them," he said, pointing out a window. "Children of the night. What music they make!"

Dracula continued up the stairs. He came to the huge spiderweb, then walked through it, not disturbing a single strand. When Renfield reached the web, he stopped, amazed by his host's feat. He paused, wondering how he could get through. He finally tore at the delicate strands, ripping the web open with his hands. A large spider, disturbed by the destruction of its home, scurried away.

As Renfield stepped through the broken web, Dracula turned toward him and spoke: "The spider spins his web for the unwary fly. Ah, the eternal struggle for life! Each living creature must have blood to live. Blood is life, Mr. Renfield."

"Well . . . I . . ." Renfield stammered, trying to understand this strange man and his eerie words. Then he continued following Dracula up the stairs.

At the top of the stairs, the Count opened a door. Renfield entered a beautifully decorated, comfortable-looking room with a roaring fire burning in its large stone fireplace.

"I'm sure you will find this part of my castle more inviting," said Dracula.

The Englishman smiled with relief. "Well, I should say so," he replied, feeling more at ease. He walked over to the fireplace. "The fire is so cheerful," he remarked. "Just the thing I need after my long journey."

"I thought you might be hungry," said Dracula, pointing to a table on the other side of the room. It was set with fine china, silver, and a crisp white-linen tablecloth. A cloth covered the dinner plate, keeping the supper warm.

"Why, thank you, sir," said Renfield. "That's very

kind of you. But I'm a bit worried about my luggage. You see, all your papers were in my briefcase, and—"

"I took the liberty of having your luggage brought to this room," explained Dracula. He pointed to Renfield's briefcase, which stood on a desk. "I trust you've kept your trip here a secret."

"Oh, yes, indeed," replied Renfield. "Just as you requested. I've followed your instructions exactly." He sat down at the desk and opened his briefcase.

"Excellent, Mr. Renfield, excellent!" The Count beamed. "And now, if you are not too tired, I would like to look at the lease for Carfax Abbey."

"Of course," said the lawyer, pulling the papers from his briefcase. "Everything is in order, awaiting your signature. Here's the lease." He handed the document to Count Dracula. "I hope I brought enough labels for your luggage."

"I am bringing only one, uh . . . box."

Renfield, surprised, pulled out a luggage label. "Very well. One it is."

"I have chartered a ship to take us to England," explained Dracula. "We will be leaving tomorrow evening."

"Everything will be ready."

Dracula walked over to a large bed near the fireplace. "I hope you'll find this comfortable," he said, pointing at the bed.

Renfield nodded gratefully. The thought of a good night's sleep was quite appealing. "Thank you. It looks very inviting."

As he started to gather the documents on the desk, Renfield cut his finger on a paper clip. "Ouch!" he cried as blood appeared on his fingertip.

At the sight of the blood, Dracula's face grew intense. His eyes narrowed. He quickly moved across the room toward his guest.

Renfield sucked the blood from his finger and pulled out a handkerchief, not noticing his host's strange reaction.

Dracula came closer, drawn by the blood. Renfield was still fumbling with his handkerchief as the Count's bony fingers reached out for his throat. At that moment Renfield looked up abruptly, and the cross that had been given him by the innkeeper's wife fell out of his shirt, dangling in front of Dracula's face.

The Count backed away, covering his face in horror.

"Oh, it's nothing serious," said Renfield, thinking his host was reacting to the wound. "Just a small cut from a paper clip." He sucked on the finger again.

Dracula turned away and struggled to control himself.

After a few moments he brought a bottle of wine and a single glass over from the table.

"This is very old wine," Dracula said, setting the glass and the wine on the desk in front of Renfield. "I hope you like it." He filled the glass and handed it to his guest, secretly slipping something into the wine.

"Aren't you drinking?" asked Renfield, taking a sip.

"I never drink . . . wine!" replied Dracula. He stared at his guest.

Renfield suddenly felt slightly dizzy. He sipped more wine, thinking it would clear his head. "It's delicious!" he said, feeling uneasy but trying to hide this fact from his host.

"And now," said Dracula, bowing, "I will leave you."

"Well, good night," said Renfield, standing.

"I may be detained elsewhere most of the day tomorrow," explained Dracula. "We will meet here tomorrow evening at sundown. Good night, Mr. Renfield." He gathered up his cape and walked out of the room.

Renfield stood and loosened his tie. What a bizarre character this Count Dracula was, he thought. Then his head suddenly became cloudy. He hadn't had much wine and wondered why he was feeling so odd.

Walking over to a set of large glass doors that led outside, he opened them to get some fresh air.

Suddenly, from out of the night mist, a large bat fluttered into the room.

Renfield grew dizzy, and the room began to spin. He grabbed his head, then fell to the floor, unconscious.

The bat hovered in the air.

Soon Dracula's three vampire wives entered the room from the other side. They had just returned from their night of drinking human blood. The women approached Renfield, who was stretched out on the floor.

The bat flew out into the night mist, and seconds later Dracula reemerged from it and entered the room. At the sight of their master, the women stopped. With a wave of his hand and a penetrating stare, Dracula commanded them to back away from the body on the floor. They obeyed and left the room.

Dracula knelt beside Renfield. He opened his cape wide, then closed it around the young lawyer's body. He dipped his head and sank his fangs into Renfield's throat, growling like an animal as he drank the Englishman's blood.

CHAPTER 3

Voyage to England

The following night a chartered ship named the *Vesta* began its long journey to London, England.

The crew thought it strange that the only cargo on board was a long wooden box, about four feet wide and seven feet long. A large tag on the side of the box declared its destination: Carfax Abbey, Whitby, in care of Count Dracula.

Even stranger to the crew than the cargo was the passenger that accompanied the box—the one passenger the crew knew about. He was a wild-eyed man who seemed in a permanent state of panic. His shoulders were hunched, and he constantly looked around as if he thought he was being watched.

The crew knew him only as "Renfield." He was the very same Renfield who had journeyed to Castle Dracula.

But the dapper young English lawyer had undergone a frightening transformation. By drinking Renfield's blood, Count Dracula had turned the lawyer into his slave. The Count, knowing he would need someone to accompany him on the long sea journey, had planned all along to turn Renfield into his servant. Now he was a nervous, twitching madman. He ate insects for their blood because he had lost so much of his own. He preferred flies, and would go out of his way to catch and eat the tiny creatures. When not feasting on insects, he lived only to serve Dracula, his new master.

During the days at sea, Count Dracula rested on the Transylvanian earth in his coffin—the wooden box he had brought on board the ship. If Renfield had not been there, Dracula would have been unprotected, and a curious crew member might have been tempted to open the box. That would have been very dangerous for Dracula, for once exposed to sunlight, his body would have burst into flames and he would have been destroyed.

Renfield spent the days of the voyage crouched next to Dracula's coffin, guarding it while catching and eating any insects he could find. Whenever a sailor happened to go down into the cargo hold, where Dracula's box was kept, Renfield screamed and gestured like a lunatic until the crewman left.

As soon as the sun set each evening, Renfield would open the lid of the coffin. Then the vampire would rise and walk the ship, unseen.

Dracula needed human blood to survive. Because of this, he had hired many more crew members than were actually needed to run the ship. Every night during the voyage, some sailor would mysteriously vanish. The crew were puzzled by these nightly disappearances, but they could come up with no explanation. They did not know that Dracula had drained the blood of the missing sailors and then thrown their bodies overboard. The disappearances remained a mystery.

With less than one day left on its voyage to London, the ship ran into a terrible storm. Wind whipped the sails and bent the masts as the sea churned, tossing the ship as if it were a toy. Waves rose up and crashed onto the deck, flooding the vessel. The crew worked feverishly to keep the *Vesta* from sinking.

Down in the cargo hold, Dracula stirred inside his coffin, for it was now nightfall.

"I hear you in there," whimpered Renfield as he lifted the lid.

Dracula sat up for a moment, then stepped out of the wooden box.

"You will keep your promise when we get to

London, won't you, master?" pleaded Renfield. "You will see that I get lives? Not human lives, but small creatures with blood in them. I'll be loyal to you, master. I'll be loyal!"

Dracula stared at the pathetic wretch, then turned and walked away without saying a word. He climbed the stairs to the *Vesta*'s deck and opened the overhead hatch. Stepping out into the storm, he saw the sailors struggling to save the ship.

Before this night is through, the Count said to himself, I will feast on the blood of these remaining crewmen.

The following morning the sailing ship *Vesta* drifted into port in London. A huge crowd gathered on the dock, staring in awe at this wrecked vessel. Its once proud masts had snapped like twigs, the sails hanging in tattered shreds, and its hull was damaged beyond repair.

"It looks like they hit a terrible storm," said someone in the crowd.

"That's the ship from Central Europe," said another.

An English police officer, known as a "bobby," tried to get the crowd to move away from the dock. "Here now," he said, "get back! Nobody but the authorities can board this boat."

The crowd moved back but continued to stare at the wreck.

"Look, the captain is dead!" cried a man in the crowd. "His hands are tied to the wheel. He must have known his ship was doomed!"

"But look at the expression on his face," said someone else in the crowd. "It looks like something frightened him to death!"

The local authorities soon arrived on the scene, led by a police inspector. They boarded the ship and were shocked by what they found.

"The crew are all dead," said the inspector. "But not from the storm! Their throats have been torn out, and all the blood has been drained from their bodies. What in the world could have happened to them?"

Suddenly, weird laughter could be heard drifting up from below the deck.

"What was that?" asked the inspector.

"It seems to be coming from that hatchway there, sir," answered his assistant, pointing to the hatchway door that led to the cargo hold.

The inspector lifted the door and saw Renfield standing at the bottom of the steps. He was laughing insanely, his eyes opened wide and gleaming with a crazy light.

"Master, master, we've arrived," he muttered. But

there was no one else in the hold, just Renfield and a large wooden box. "Master, can you hear me? We're here. We're safe!"

"Why, he's mad!" exclaimed the inspector. "Just look at his eyes. And listen to him talking to himself. He's crazy!"

Renfield was taken to the Seward Sanitarium, a famous psychiatric hospital located in the town of Whitby, near London. The staff at the sanitarium, shocked and repulsed by the new inmate's craving to eat flies, ants, and other small living things, held him there for observation.

The box on board the *Vesta* was sent to the address on its tag—Carfax Abbey, in care of Count Dracula. It was delivered to the abbey that afternoon.

And as the sun set that evening, Dracula rose from his coffin and prepared to spend his first night in London.

The thick night fog for which London was famous shrouded the busy city streets. Taxi horns and other sounds of night traffic filled the air. Pedestrians shouted at one another as they made their way to theaters and restaurants, or journeyed home from work.

Count Dracula strolled through this bustling

scene. He loved big, crowded, noisy cities, where it was easy to find victims—and easy to escape after dispatching them. In Transylvania local peasants always warned new visitors of the dangers that lurked outside in the night. But in London, Dracula knew, he could easily fade into a crowd. After all, crime was not unusual in a big city like London, and a few more murders would not be noticed.

The Count moved through the thickening fog, his formal clothes crowned by a tall black top hat. He looked like a typical London gentleman out for a night on the town.

On a street corner a young girl sold flowers from a tray. "Violets!" she called to the pedestrians rushing past. "Flower, sir? Flower, madam?"

Dracula, suddenly emerging from the fog, stepped up to the flower girl.

"A flower for your cape, sir?" she asked.

The Count nodded. The girl reached over and pinned a violet onto his cape. When she looked at Dracula, she was frightened by the glow of his eerie red eyes. But she was hypnotized by his stare and could not turn away.

Feeling dizzy, she suddenly fainted. As she slumped to the ground, Dracula caught her in his powerful grasp. The fog closed in around them as the vampire brought his sharp fangs toward her neck.

When he had drained the girl of her blood, he let her body slump to the ground. He disappeared into the crowd to watch what would happen next. Soon a bobby's whistle sounded. Dracula glanced over his shoulder and saw several policemen rushing to the corner where he had left the flower seller.

A crowd had gathered around the lifeless girl. The first bobby to reach the corner pushed his way through the crowd and knelt next to the victim. Several other bobbies ran up from different directions. When they reached the crowd, they realized they were too late. One of the policemen picked up the girl's limp body in his arms and carried her away.

Dracula turned and started walking. Soon he came to a theater. Men in silk top hats and women in lavish evening gowns were gathered together under the brilliantly lit marquee, exchanging greetings. Dracula paused in front of the theater for a moment. Then he removed his top hat and stepped inside.

CHAPTER 4
Count Dracula in London

The theater lobby was beautifully decorated. Its high ceiling was trimmed with gold-painted molding, the walls were covered with colorful murals depicting London street life. Elegant townspeople paused to admire the exquisite lobby before moving on to find their seats. They had come to listen to a performance by the London Symphony Orchestra.

The lights in the lobby flashed three times, a signal that the performance was about to begin. Count Dracula made his way into the auditorium, handing his ticket stub to an usher. She shined her flashlight on the stub and whispered, "Right this way, sir. Follow me."

Then the house lights dimmed, and the conductor tapped his baton on his music stand. He raised his arms, and the concert began.

Dr. Seward, who ran the sanitarium where Renfield had been taken, was seated with his party in one of the private boxes facing the stage. The doctor was a tall, distinguished-looking gentleman with a thin, pointed face and graying hair that he combed straight back.

Next to Dr. Seward sat Lucy Weston, a longtime friend of the Seward family. She was dressed in a beautiful evening gown, and her long blond hair fell down to her shoulders in curls. Lucy was smiling, listening to the lovely music.

Also in the box were Mina Seward, the doctor's daughter, and her fiancé, Jonathan Harker. Harker's arm was draped over the back of Mina's seat. Mina smiled at Jonathan, moving her hand over to his. He returned the smile and took her hand. It was obvious to anyone who saw them together that they were very much in love.

Dracula followed the usher to an area behind the theater's private boxes. At the door to Dr. Seward's box, he handed the usher his hat and cape, which she hung on a nearby hook. As she turned back to the Count, he stared deeply into her eyes, waving his hand in front of her face. The usher's eyes went blank, and then her arms dropped to her sides.

Dracula moved in closer. "You will go into Dr. Seward's box and deliver a message," he commanded.

She continued to stare blankly at him.

"You will tell the doctor that there is a telephone call for him," Dracula continued. "After you deliver the message, you will not remember this conversation. You will forget that you ever saw me. You will obey."

"I will obey," said the usher in a mechanical voice.

Just then there was a short break in the music, and the house lights came back on. As the audience applauded loudly, the usher entered Dr. Seward's box. "Excuse me, Dr. Seward," she said in the same mechanical voice. "You are wanted on the telephone."

The doctor nodded, then stood to leave the box. "Will you excuse me?" he said to his guests.

"Oh, Father," began Mina, "I forgot to ask you. May I spend the night here in town with Lucy?"

"All right, dear," replied her father. "That will be fine."

Seward parted the curtains leading to the box's exit. As he started to leave, Count Dracula stepped up to the curtains from the hallway beyond.

"Pardon me, sir," said the Count in his most regal tone, "but I could not help overhearing your name. Are you the Dr. Seward whose sanitarium is at Whitby?"

"Why, yes!" said the doctor, sounding surprised.

"Please allow me to introduce myself," the vampire said, bowing slightly. "I am Count Dracula. I've just leased Carfax Abbey. I understand it borders the grounds of your sanitarium."

"Why, yes, it does," replied Dr. Seward in a friendly tone. "I'm very happy to meet you, sir." He turned back toward the others in his box. "Allow me to present my daughter, Mina," Seward said. "And this is Miss Lucy Weston and Mr. Jonathan Harker."

Dracula bowed gracefully.

"Count Dracula has just taken over Carfax Abbey," Seward continued. "He's going to be our neighbor."

"It'll be a relief to see lights burning in those dismal old windows," said Mina.

"It will indeed," added her father. "Now if you'll excuse me, everyone, I'm wanted on the telephone." He pointed toward an empty seat in the box. "Count Dracula, won't you join us?"

"Thank you!" replied Dracula graciously. "I'd be delighted."

When Dr. Seward had left, Harker spoke to the Count. "I should think the abbey could be made quite attractive, but it's going to need some rather extensive repairs."

"Actually, I intend to keep it the way it is now,"

explained Dracula. "In its current state it reminds me of my own castle in Transylvania."

Lucy Weston loved visiting exotic places and meeting interesting people of other cultures. Although she had never been to Transylvania, she was fascinated by this charming man and was now suddenly infatuated with him. "The abbey always reminds me of that old rhyme," she said, staring directly at Dracula. "The one that goes, 'Lofty timbers, the walls around are bare. Echoing to our laughter, as though the dead were there.'"

"Nice little sentiment," grunted Harker sarcastically.

"But wait, there's more," continued Lucy. "And it's even nicer: 'Lift your cup for the dead already, hurrah for the next to die. And if—'"

"Never mind the rest, dear," interrupted Mina. She found this eerie old rhyme frightening and didn't want to hear how it ended.

Count Dracula thought about what he had heard. Because he had walked the earth for centuries, the thought of actually dying brought a strange smile to his lips. "To die," he said softly, almost to himself. "To really be dead. That must be glorious."

Mina was shocked. "Why, Count Dracula, I—"

"There are far worse things awaiting man than death, Miss Mina," the Count said, interrupting her.

The house lights dimmed again, and the conversation ended. After the music resumed, Dracula stared at Lucy, feeling her fascination for him. This one would be easy, he thought. Then he settled back in his seat and listened to the orchestra.

After the concert Mina went home with Lucy. Mina always enjoyed staying at her friend's town house, for she found being in London exciting, so different from her quiet life in the small town of Whitby. Both women were looking forward to the shopping excursion they had planned for the next day.

Now Mina sat on the edge of Lucy's bed, talking to her friend, who was sitting at her dressing table.

Lucy was imitating Count Dracula's voice and manner. "'It reminds me of my own castle in Transylvania,'" she said, catching the Count's accent and tone perfectly. Then she sighed and looked at Mina.

Mina laughed. "Oh, Lucy," she began, "you're so romantic!"

"Laugh all you want to," replied Lucy, picking up a comb and running it through her hair. "I thought he was fascinating!"

"I suppose he's all right," said Mina, shrugging. "But give me someone a little . . . well, more normal."

"Like John?" asked her friend, smiling.

"Yes," responded Mina. "Like John."

Lucy stared out the window beside her dressing table and sighed deeply once more. "Give me a ruined old castle," she mused, "a gentleman count, and the mysterious country of Transylvania." She sighed again, lost in her own thoughts.

Mina got up from the bed and walked over to the dressing table. "Well, Countess Lucy of Transylvania," she said playfully, "I'm sleepy. I'll leave you to your count and his ruined abbey. I hope you have very pleasant dreams."

"Good night, Mina," said Lucy, still lost in thought.

"Good night," said Mina, opening the bedroom door. "See you in the morning." Closing the door behind her, she headed for the guest room down the hall.

Lucy walked to the window and opened it slightly, then stared out at the foggy night, imagining herself in the mountains of Transylvania.

Just below her window, under a fog-shrouded streetlamp, Count Dracula stood quietly, his long black cape billowing in the chilly night breeze.

A bobby on his evening rounds strolled past him, remarking, "Looks like the fog is closing in again, sir."

Dracula nodded.

The bobby gazed curiously at Dracula, looking back as he moved on down the street.

As soon as the policeman had disappeared from view, Dracula looked up at Lucy's window.

Inside, the young woman gazed at the London night for a few more seconds, then turned back into her room, leaving the window open. She crawled under her soft quilted comforter and picked up a book from her night table.

Just beyond the bedroom window, the fog grew denser. Suddenly a large bat flew out of the fog and circled outside. It hovered in place, watching Lucy grow drowsy and put her book aside. She turned off her reading lamp and closed her eyes, smiling slightly before slipping into a pleasant dream.

As soon as Lucy was asleep, the bat flew into her bedroom. There it underwent an incredible transformation.

In place of the bat stood the tall, sinister figure of Count Dracula.

Dracula slowly advanced toward Lucy. He moved silently, like an animal stalking its prey, each step bringing him closer to his sleeping victim.

When he reached the head of the bed, the Count extended his long, bony fingers and parted his lips, exposing his sharp white fangs. Then he let out a wolfish growl and stared at Lucy's unconcious form.

Finally he lowered his head slowly toward Lucy's exposed throat.

The following morning Mina discovered Lucy's unconscious body. After Mina called for help, Lucy was rushed to a nearby London hospital.

Bright sunshine streamed in through a skylight in the hospital's operating room, glistening off its clean white walls and chrome tables. But the mood in the room was gloomy, in stark contrast to the sunshine outside.

Dr. Seward stood next to the surgeons gathered around the operating table, observing Lucy's motionless body. The senior surgeon shook his head grimly, then pulled a white sheet up over Lucy's face.

"I'm sorry, Dr. Seward," said the surgeon. "Miss Weston is dead."

Seward was visibly shaken.

"I have seen several other cases exactly like this one in the past twelve hours," explained the surgeon. "They all go beyond my understanding. All the deaths have had the same cause: an unnatural loss of blood, with no major wound to explain it." He pulled out a magnifying glass and pulled back the sheet, then leaned in toward Lucy's neck, bringing the magnifying glass up to his eye. "These same two puncture marks have been found on all the victims' necks!"

Dr. Seward looked at the two tiny red marks on Lucy's neck, shuddering in horror.

CHAPTER 5
Vampire Hunter!

Professor Van Helsing was the most respected scientist in Austria, and his reputation extended throughout Europe. He worked in a modern laboratory situated high in the Austrian mountains, not far from Dracula's native Transylvania.

His laboratory was huge, with a high ceiling that arched over long worktables. On the tables stood racks of test tubes, bottles, and small burners. One entire wall was lined with scientific volumes containing centuries of knowledge. The opposite wall of the laboratory had a huge picture window that looked out on the mountains.

Professor Van Helsing was a short, white-haired man of about sixty, whose thick, wire-framed glasses gave him an impressive, intelligent look. He was a dedicated scientist—rational, logical, very up to date.

But his passion was the study of vampires. He knew better than most people that the strange, superstitious legends of supposedly ignorant peasants were more than just stories, for he had chased vampires from one end of Europe to the other. He had even killed a few of them by driving sharp wooden stakes through their hearts. Even so, there were many who thought him insane for pursuing creatures they believed did not exist.

This particular morning Van Helsing had several guests, including Dr. Seward and the English surgeon who had tried to save Lucy Weston. They had traveled from England to consult the professor, having been told that he might be able to help them solve the mystery surrounding the bizarre deaths of Lucy and several other women in London.

The professor peered through his thick lenses at a sample of blood in a test tube, which he held over a flame rising from a burner. He removed the heated blood sample from the flame, then added a chemical from a nearby bottle.

All eyes in the room stared intently at the test tube. As the chemical was added, the hot blood turned milky white!

Van Helsing now took a single drop of the white liquid and placed it on a clear glass slide. He dropped a tiny square of glass over the sample, then placed the slide under his microscope. As the two doctors leaned over his shoulder, Van Helsing looked into the microscope. He straightened up after studying the slide for a few seconds, then turned to face the other men, his expression grim. "Gentlemen," he said softly, "we are dealing with the undead."

Dr. Seward and the surgeon exchanged glances of horror. "The undead?" asked Seward, unable to hide his shock.

"Yes, the undead," replied Van Helsing, nodding gravely. "In other words, vampires! Vampires attack the throats of their victims. They leave two little round puncture marks, just like the ones you observed on Lucy and the others."

Seward and the surgeon looked at each other. This vampire story would explain the unnatural loss of blood from all the victims. But vampires were not real, thought Seward. The very idea of vampires seemed impossible.

"Dr. Seward," Van Helsing continued, "you have told me that your patient Renfield is obsessed with the idea that he must eat living things in order to sustain his own life. This obsession is also the result of a vampire's bite."

"But, Professor," objected the surgeon, "modern medical science doesn't admit the existence of such creatures. Vampires are pure myth and superstition!"

The professor's face hardened. Another fool who refuses to believe, he thought to himself. "I may be able to furnish you with proof, Doctor," he stated. "Proof that the superstition of yesterday can become the scientific reality of today!"

His guests looked at him questioningly.

"I will come with you to England," Van Helsing explained. "I will go to Dr. Seward's sanitarium and observe Renfield myself. I am sure that I will stand face-to-face with that dark and dangerous creature of the night—the vampire!"

Dr. Seward and Mina lived in the main building of the Seward Sanitarium. The patients and staff were housed in two wings that extended from the sides of the Sewards' home.

It was a peaceful place on this late afternoon. Flower-lined paths ran the length of the property, and bushes and trees were tastefully scattered around the grassy grounds. Some patients strolled over these pathways. A few sat under shade trees, reading, while others were pushed in wheelchairs by the sanitarium's nurses and attendants.

Suddenly the calm was shattered by a bloodcurdling scream from inside.

"That's Renfield again," said a patient outside. "He probably wants some more flies to eat!"

Renfield was kept in the patient wing of the sanitarium, in a small room with barred windows. The furnishings were a single hospital bed, one dresser, and a chair.

Martin, the attendant assigned to Renfield, was now inside this room struggling with his crazed charge.

Renfield pulled his hands close to his chest, attempting to keep something from the attendant. Martin grabbed the patient's hands, trying to pry them open.

"Oh, Martin, please," cried Renfield pitifully. "Don't take him away from me. Please don't, please!"

Martin finally succeeded in prying open Renfield's hands, removing a large spider that the madman had been clutching. Renfield let out a mournful wail that could be heard throughout the sanitarium.

"Spiders now, is it?" said Martin, ignoring his charge and looking at the creature wriggling in his hand. "Flies aren't good enough for you anymore, eh? Aren't you ashamed?" He went to the window and tossed the spider out between the steel bars.

Renfield stopped crying and glared at Martin. "Flies!" he exclaimed with contempt. "Poor puny flies! Who wants to eat flies?"

"You do, you blasted loony!" barked the attendant

in disbelief. He had been watching Renfield eat flies since the lunatic had arrived at the sanitarium.

"No flies!" said Renfield. His eyes opened wide and a demented smile crossed his face. "Not when I can get nice, fat, juicy spiders!"

Martin shrugged and shook his head. "All right," he replied, "have it your way. No flies." He took Renfield by the arm and led him from the room. "Come along, now," he said forcefully. "Dr. Seward is waiting to talk to you again."

Dr. Seward's office was clean and bright, furnished with the most up-to-date equipment available. His desk sat near a large window that looked out onto the sanitarium's grounds.

He was sitting at this desk as Professor Van Helsing paced back and forth in front of the window. The two of them were discussing the strange case of Renfield.

"Professor," Seward said, "Renfield craves only small living things. He is not interested in anything human."

Van Helsing stopped pacing and turned to face Seward. "This is true only as far as we know, Doctor," explained the professor. "But you tell me he escapes from his room. You said that sometimes he is gone for hours. Where does he go, and what does he do during that time? When I first saw him this morning, he looked like a madman, capable of—"

The professor was interrupted by the sound of the door opening. Martin and Renfield entered the room. The patient looked quite normal as he stepped quietly forward, nodding at the two men.

Van Helsing walked over to Renfield and extended his hand. "Well, Mr. Renfield," the professor said in a very friendly voice, "you look much better than you did when we met this morning."

Renfield nodded politely. "Thank you, Professor Van Helsing," he replied. "I'm feeling much better." He sat down.

"I'm here to help you," said the professor. "You understand that, don't you?"

"Why, of course," answered Renfield. "I'm really very grateful."

Van Helsing, thinking some actual progress had been made, walked over to Renfield and placed a comforting hand on his shoulder.

At the touch of Van Helsing's hand, Renfield jumped from his seat and screamed, "Keep your filthy hands to yourself!"

Martin moved forward at this sudden outburst, ready to protect the professor from a possible attack. Martin knew that Renfield could become violent at any moment.

"Now, now, Renfield," said Dr. Seward, trying to calm his patient.

At the sound of the doctor's voice, Renfield turned and began to plead with him. "Oh, Dr. Seward!" he cried. "I want you to send me away from this place. Send me far away!"

"Why are you so anxious to get away?" asked Professor Van Helsing.

Renfield turned back to the professor. "My cries at night, they might disturb Miss Mina. They might give her bad dreams. Very bad dreams!"

Outside, a wolf howled. Renfield, visibly shaken by the sound, rushed to the window and saw that the sun had just set. He knew that in the nearby abbey Dracula had just risen from his coffin.

"That sounded like a wolf," commented Van Helsing.

"Why, yes, it did," said Dr. Seward. "But I hardly think there are wolves this close to London!"

Martin pointed at Renfield, who was huddled near the window, listening carefully. "He thinks there are wolves," said the attendant. "He thinks they are talking to him. In fact, he howls back at them. He's crazy, you know!"

"I might have known," said Van Helsing, walking over to Renfield. "We know why the wolves talk, don't we, Mr. Renfield?" Van Helsing reached into his pocket. "And we know how we can stop them, don't we?"

Van Helsing pulled out a sprig of wolfsbane and shoved it under Renfield's nose. The lunatic sprang back, glaring at the professor.

"You know too much to live, Van Helsing!" shouted Renfield, his fury growing. Then he continued to snarl and rant.

Van Helsing moved back to the desk, a satisfied smile on his face. "We won't get any more out of him for a while now," he said.

"Take him away, Martin," ordered Dr. Seward.

"Let's get moving, fly-eater!" Martin cried, yanking Renfield by the arm.

"I'm warning you, Dr. Seward!" yelled Renfield as they reached the door. "If you don't send me away, you must answer for what happens to Miss Mina!"

Martin pulled Renfield from the doctor's office and took him back to his room.

"What's that herb that excited him so?" the doctor asked when Renfield was gone.

"Wolfsbane," explained Van Helsing. "It's a plant that grows in Central Europe. I brought some with me. The natives there use it to protect themselves from vampires!"

"Renfield reacted very violently to its scent," Dr. Seward remarked.

"A vampire here in England has control over Renfield," said Van Helsing. "Our fly-eating friend must be watched all the time. But especially at night!"

CHAPTER 6
The Vampire's Victim

After leaving Dr. Seward and the others, Renfield paced back and forth in his room like a caged animal. When he grew tired, he stretched out on his bed, tossing restlessly. Frightening thoughts flooded his head. He knew that it was only a matter of time before Dracula returned. Would his master be angry that he had warned Dr. Seward about Mina?

Suddenly the wolf howled, sending a chill through Renfield. He bounded up from his bed and rushed to the window. Below, staring up at him, stood Count Dracula. Even from this distance, the vampire was able to lock on to Renfield's eyes.

"Yes, master," said Renfield, hypnotized by the Count's stare. "Master, you've come back. I'm pleased."

Using his mental hold over his servant, Dracula sent Renfield a silent message.

"No, master!" cried Renfield in response to the message. "Please don't, master! Not her! No, not her!"

Dracula turned abruptly, ignoring his creature's pleas, and disappeared into the darkness. Renfield sank down onto his bed, burying his head in his hands and beginning to sob.

A full moon shone in the night sky. As it was an unusually warm evening, Mina decided to sleep with her bedroom window open. She had just put her book aside and was beginning to drift off into a deep slumber when she heard a howling outside. She opened her eyes and saw that the room was filled with a thick mist. Thinking she was dreaming, she closed her eyes again, then slept fitfully.

Suddenly a large bat flew through the open window—the same bat that had come to Lucy. And now, once again, the furry winged creature transformed itself into Count Dracula.

He approached Mina's bed, pulling his cape around him, just as a bat pulls in its wings. Seeing that she slept, Dracula smiled. She would have a dream tonight, he thought. One she would never forget.

He opened his cape wide now and leaned down over the bed, his eyes burning red and his sharp fangs sticking out from his mouth. Then he lowered his head down toward Mina's throat.

When Mina awoke the next morning, her memories of the night before seemed like nothing more than a terrifying dream. Still, for the next few days she was not quite herself. If anyone asked her how she was, however, she said she was fine.

Nevertheless, she felt strangely different. At first she did not want to tell anyone about the dream. But as the days and restless nights passed, she could no longer keep it to herself.

Several nights after the attack, she finally decided to discuss her frightening experience with her fiancé, Jonathan Harker. They met in the library, a comfortable room in the Sewards' living quarters. Harker lit a fire and sat on the sofa next to Mina. "You just tell me all about this dream, my dear," he said.

Mina, looking exhausted and nervous, began her story. "I was up in bed for a short while, reading. Just as I began to feel drowsy, I heard a dog howling. I must have fallen asleep then, because the room seemed to fill with mist."

Unseen by Mina or Harker, Dr. Seward and Professor Van Helsing had appeared at the library door and were standing there listening to Mina's story.

"The mist was so thick," she continued, "that I couldn't see a thing. Even the light from my lamp seemed like a tiny spark in the fog.

"And then I saw two glowing red eyes staring at me through the mist. A horrible white face, like that of some strange animal, looked down at me."

Seward and Van Helsing exchanged startled looks, then stepped into the room as Mina went on with her story.

"It came closer and closer to me," she said, becoming more agitated. "I felt its foul breath on my face. And its lips—oh, John!" She broke off her story with a shudder and covered her face with her hands.

Harker looked up and noticed that Seward and Van Helsing had joined them. He started to speak, but Van Helsing held up his hand as if to say, "Let her finish."

Harker took Mina by the hand and tried to comfort her. "But, dear, it was only a dream. You mustn't—"

"When I awoke from the dream the next morning," she interrupted, ignoring him, "I felt weak, as if all life had been drained out of me."

"Darling, we're going to forget all about this dream," said Harker. "Let's think about something happy, shall we?"

Mina looked up at him and, pressing his hand against her cheek, tried to smile. Harker sighed heavily, hoping that she would forget about this terrible nightmare.

Van Helsing crossed over to the sofa. "May I speak with Miss Mina?" he asked Harker.

"Certainly, Professor," Harker replied, getting up from the sofa.

Van Helsing sat down next to Mina. "Think for a moment," he began in a soothing voice. "Is there anything that might have brought this dream on?"

The girl thought for a moment. "No," she replied.

Harker, standing next to Dr. Seward, leaned toward him and whispered, "There's something else troubling Mina. It's not just her dream. I think there's something she doesn't want to tell us."

"I don't understand," said the doctor, puzzled.

Van Helsing continued questioning Mina. "The face in this dream—you say it came closer and closer?"

Mina nodded.

"And the lips touched you?"

Again she nodded. This time a shiver ran down her spine.

"Where did they touch you?" asked the professor. Without waiting for an answer, he reached for the scarf Mina wore around her neck.

Mina's own hand flew to her neck, as if protecting it from the professor. "No, please," she pleaded.

"Is there something wrong with your throat?" Van Helsing asked.

"No . . . I mean, I'm not sure," stammered Mina.

"Permit me, please, Miss Mina," said the professor. He removed the scarf and, pulling a magnifying glass from his pocket, examined her neck. There he discovered two small puncture marks.

"How long have you had these little marks on your neck?" he asked.

"Since the morning after the dream," she said, shaken.

"Mina, dear, why didn't you let us know right away?" asked Harker, obviously alarmed at this discovery.

The girl remained silent. Something—some force she couldn't identify—had kept her from telling the others about the wounds right away. If it had not been for Van Helsing's insistence, she would never have revealed these marks to anyone.

"What could have caused these marks, Professor?" asked Harker.

"Count Dracula!" announced a voice that was not the professor's.

A maid had entered the room, interrupting the conversation. "Count Dracula is here," she repeated.

Dracula strode into the library. "Good evening," he said. "It's good to see you again, Doctor."

"Good evening," said Dr. Seward, distracted. He was preoccupied by his daughter's condition and did not welcome this unexpected visit.

Dracula turned to Mina. "And you, Miss Mina," he continued. "You are looking exceptionally—" He noticed the somber mood of the room, which seemed to center upon Mina. "Oh, I'm sorry, Miss Mina," he said in a false tone of concern. "Are you ill?"

"You'll pardon me, Doctor," Van Helsing said impatiently, "but I think Miss Seward should go to her room at once."

Dracula turned swiftly and looked directly at this stranger. Although he did not know the man, he was instantly uncomfortable in his presence.

"In that case," said Dracula graciously, "I will not stay." He turned to Mina. "It's nothing serious, I hope?"

"Oh, please don't go," Mina said to Dracula. She was glad he had interrupted them, for she had been uncomfortable discussing the wounds on her neck. "I'm sure it's not as important as Professor Van Helsing seems to think."

Dracula stared at Van Helsing.

Dr. Seward suddenly realized the two men had never met. "Forgive me," he said. "Count Dracula, this is Professor Van Helsing."

Van Helsing bowed stiffly.

"Van Helsing," Dracula said, bowing as well. "Yours is a name we know even in the wilds of Transylvania. You are a most distinguished scientist." Then he moved toward Mina.

"I had a frightful dream a few nights ago," she said to the Count. "I haven't been able to get it out of my mind."

"I hope you haven't been taking my stories too seriously," said Dracula.

"Stories?" snapped Harker, jealous.

"I've been telling your fiancée some rather grim tales of my far-off country," the Count explained.

"I can imagine," Harker shot back, the annoyance in his voice clear.

"Why, John," scolded Mina. "That wasn't very polite. After all, Count Dracula is our neighbor. He has entertained me with his stories on several occasions."

"I'm sorry," apologized Harker. "I didn't mean to be rude."

"Of course not," replied Dracula politely. "I can quite understand Mr. Harker's concern, Miss Mina."

Van Helsing, bored with this conversation, lifted the lid of an antique wooden box that was filled with small candies. A mirror lined the inside of the lid. He was reaching for one of the candies when he noticed something remarkable.

The mirror in the lid picked up the reflection of the group gathered around the sofa. Van Helsing could clearly see Mina, who was seated. He also saw Dr. Seward and Harker, who were standing near her. But where was Count Dracula? he wondered.

Van Helsing turned away from the mirror and looked over at the group. Count Dracula was standing between Seward and Harker. The professor turned back to the mirror. There was no reflection of Count Dracula! This could mean just one thing, but it could also explain quite a number of others. Van Helsing once again focused his attention on the conversation.

"My dear," Seward said to his daughter, "you must go to your room as Professor Van Helsing suggests. I'm sure Count Dracula will excuse you."

"But, Father," Mina protested, "I'm feeling all right now."

Dracula stared into the girl's eyes. He said, "Your father is right. You should go to your room."

Mina's tone changed immediately. "Very well," she said. "Good night, Count Dracula."

The Count bowed. "I'll be going as well," he announced. He turned toward Van Helsing. "Professor, I hope to have the pleasure of seeing you again." He looked back at Mina and said, "I shall call again soon to inquire how you are feeling."

"Thank you, Count Dracula," she replied almost mechanically. She nodded to the others, then went up the stairs to her room.

"I'm sorry my visit was so ill-timed," Dracula apologized as soon as Mina had left.

"On the contrary, Count," said Van Helsing quickly. "It may prove to be most enlightening. In fact, before you leave, you can be of definite service to me."

"Anything I can do, I will do gladly," Dracula replied.

Dr. Seward eyed Van Helsing curiously, wondering what the professor was up to.

"A moment ago I stumbled upon an amazing phenomenon," Van Helsing explained. "Something so incredible that I mistrust my own judgment." He lifted the wooden candy box. "I want you to help me prove something." He snapped open the lid of the box, revealing the mirror, then thrust it at Dracula as if it were a weapon. "Look!" he shouted.

Dracula, his face twisted with rage, snarled like an animal being attacked. He grabbed the box from Van Helsing, then threw it on the floor, smashing the mirror to pieces.

Van Helsing looked on with a satisfied smile. Seward and Harker were frozen with shock.

The Count tried to regain control of himself. "Dr. Seward," he began, trying to think of some rational explanation he could give for his outburst, "my humble apologies. I dislike mirrors. Professor Van Helsing no doubt can explain." He turned and stared menacingly at Van Helsing. "For one who has not yet lived even a single lifetime, you are a wise man, Professor."

Van Helsing was quivering with excitement. He

kept his smile in place, however, and met the Count's stare.

Dracula, furious, turned and quickly left the house through the double french doors that led from the library out onto the patio.

"What could have caused that?" asked Harker. "Did you see the look on his face? He was like a wild animal!" He moved to the french doors and looked out onto the sanitarium's fog-covered grounds. "What's that?" he shouted, pointing. "Something is running across the lawn. It looks like a huge dog!"

"Or a wolf?" asked Van Helsing knowingly.

"A wolf!" exclaimed Harker, turning away from the doors.

"He was afraid we might follow him, so he took the form of a wolf," Van Helsing explained. "But more often, they take the form of bats."

"I don't understand," said Harker. "What in the world are you talking about?"

"Dracula," stated Van Helsing. "I'm talking about Count Dracula."

"But what has Dracula got to do with wolves and bats?" Seward asked.

Van Helsing, facing Seward and Harker, spoke in a very serious voice. "Gentlemen," he said. "Count Dracula is our vampire!"

Harker and Dr. Seward looked at Van Helsing as if

he were mad. "But surely, Professor—" Seward began, shocked that the professor would make such a completely irrational remark.

"Look at the facts, Doctor," interrupted Van Helsing. "Vampires cast no reflections in mirrors. When I held the mirror up to Dracula, he cast no reflection. That's why he smashed the box: He was furious that I had discovered his secret."

"But that doesn't make sense!" cried Harker.

Van Helsing grew angry. Once again the fools didn't want to believe the truth! "Dracula is responsible for Lucy Weston's death," he stated firmly. "And he is responsible for those puncture wounds on Miss Mina's neck!"

"I don't mean to be rude, Professor," began Harker, "but that's the sort of nonsense I'd expect from one of the patients here!"

"Yes," said Van Helsing slowly. "And yours is the reaction I expect to receive when I speak the truth. But that is the strength of vampires: People refuse to believe in them!"

CHAPTER 7
Under the Vampire's Spell

Mina again slept restlessly that night, tossing and turning as the strange dream returned and filled her head with images of bats and wolves. Sometimes she was not sure if she was awake or asleep.

And then she heard the voice.

It seemed to be coming from inside her own head, soft at first and then louder, as if someone controlled her thoughts and was using them to call her name. "Mina!" came the voice. "Mina, come to me."

The girl rose from her bed, put on a robe, and walked from her bedroom.

Moving like a zombie and staring straight ahead, she walked down the main hallway, still hearing the voice, compelled to follow its command. She stepped out the front door and made her way slowly across the sanitarium's lawn.

DRACULA

Count Dracula was waiting for her in the shadows beneath a large tree, his huge black cape wrapped tightly around him, his white face clearly visible in the dark night. Mina approached him. Dracula opened his arms, his cape unraveling like two giant bat wings. Mina, in a trance, stepped into his arms. Then Dracula closed his cape around her and pulled her off into the shadows to drink her blood.

In the sanitarium's library, Dr. Seward and Harker were still arguing with Van Helsing. Seward could not believe that their charming new neighbor was a vampire, that he was responsible for the death of Lucy Weston and for Mina's unusual behavior.

Jonathan Harker did not believe vampires existed at all. "Come now, Professor," he insisted, "vampires exist only in stories."

Once again Van Helsing tried to explain what he knew was the truth. "A vampire, Mr. Harker," he began patiently, "is a fiend who lives on, after his death, by drinking the blood of the living. It must drink blood or it dies. Its power lasts only from sunset to sunrise. During the hours of the day, it must rest in the earth in which it was buried!"

"If Dracula is indeed a vampire," interrupted Dr. Seward, "wouldn't he have to return to Transylvanian soil every night? That, of course, is impossible!"

Van Helsing, deep in thought, paced back and forth across the library. Finally he turned and faced the others. "There is only one logical explanation," he said. "Dracula must have brought at least one box of his native soil with him. A box large enough for him to sleep in."

Suddenly, insane laughter filled the room. It was Renfield, who was standing at the library door and cackling wildly.

"Renfield!" shouted Dr. Seward. "What are you doing here? You've escaped from your room again, haven't you?"

"Did you hear what we were talking about?" asked Van Helsing.

"Yes, I heard," answered Renfield. "I heard enough." Pointing at Van Helsing, he exclaimed, "Be guided by what the professor says! It is your only hope." Then he looked at Harker and added, "And it is Miss Mina's only hope." He turned to Dr. Seward. "I begged you to send me away. But you wouldn't. Now it's too late. It's happened again!"

"What's happened?" asked Harker impatiently.

Renfield turned back to Harker. "Take her away from here!" he shouted. "Take her away before—"

He was cut off by the loud, piercing shriek of a large bat that hovered just outside the open window. Then the creature flew inside, swooping down and nearly grazing the top of Renfield's head. Renfield ducked to avoid the squealing beast, then remained crouched in the corner, sniveling.

"Master! Master!" he cried in a voice filled with terror. "I wasn't going to say anything!"

The bat circled the room once more, then flew out the window. Renfield ran after it, waving his arms in a wild panic. "I told them nothing!" he screamed. "I'm loyal to you, master! I'm loyal!" He fell to his knees and buried his face in his hands, sobbing hysterically. He knew that he really had betrayed his master and that a terrible punishment would follow.

Van Helsing stepped up to Renfield and placed his hand on the sobbing man's shoulder. "What have you to do with Dracula?" the professor asked.

Renfield flinched. He was determined to give these men no more help, for he was in enough trouble with his master already. "Dracula?" he snarled. "I've never even heard the name before!"

Van Helsing frowned. "You'll die in torment if you die with innocent blood on your soul," he said. "For your own good, help us save Miss Mina!"

Renfield stood up, his eyes red from crying. "God will not damn the soul of a poor lunatic," he sobbed. "He knows the powers of evil are too great. Those with weak minds cannot resist them."

Suddenly a maid ran into the room. "Mr.

Harker!" she cried hysterically, her voice choked with emotion. "Oh, Mr. Harker, it's awful!"

She turned to Seward. "Oh, Dr. Seward, it's Miss Mina," she continued, pointing out the window to the lawn below. "Miss Mina, she's out there—dead!"

Harker, Seward, and Van Helsing dashed from the room, leaving the maid alone with Renfield.

As soon as the others were gone, he turned to the maid and began laughing in a low, eerie voice. The maid, looking at him, fainted and collapsed on the floor.

Renfield sank to his knees by her unconscious body, trying to grab a fly that had landed on her cheek. The fly got away, however, and Renfield let out a deep sigh of frustration.

Outside, on the sanitarium's lawn, Harker reached Mina's body first. "Mina!" he cried. "Oh, Mina!"

Dr. Seward knelt over the body and felt for a pulse. "She's alive!" he exclaimed. "Hurry, let's get her inside."

Harker carried Mina's limp body as they walked back toward the house.

"Thank heaven she's alive," said Seward, still shaken. "But I don't know how much more of this I can stand!"

"She may be alive," explained Van Helsing, "but

she's still in great danger. She is already under his influence!"

Behind a large maple tree in the center of the lawn, Dracula—his eyes blazing red and an evil smile on his lips—watched as the group entered the house.

"This whole thing is horrible, Van Helsing," said Seward when they were inside.

"Horrible, yes," replied the professor. "But we must face the truth, and we must do something about it. If these attacks on Mina continue, she will come more and more under Dracula's spell. Finally she will die. And then she will walk the earth at night, as one of the undead!"

CHAPTER 8
The Woman in White

The next night, in the town of Whitby, not far from Dr. Seward's sanitarium, the local police constable was riding his bicycle along a dirt road that passed the Whitby cemetery.

Suddenly he heard the sound of a child crying. Stopping his bike, he dashed off into the cemetery. He pulled out a flashlight and began searching around the headstones.

He soon found a little boy, who was sitting on the ground and crying softly to himself. "There, there, young man," said the constable. "What's wrong? And what in the world are you doing here?"

He lifted the boy up and brushed him off, then wiped the tears from his face and listened while the child told his story.

"I was just going down the road from my house to

visit a friend," the boy said, "when I saw this beautiful woman dressed in white. She told me she had some nice candy for me, so I followed her. When we came to the cemetery, I was afraid. But before I could say anything, she bent down and bit me! Then she ran away!"

"Bit you?" said the constable. "Where?"

The boy pointed to his neck. There the constable saw two small puncture wounds. "Better get you home so you can get those cleaned up," he said, leading the boy away.

As soon as the constable and the boy had left the cemetery, Lucy Weston—her long white dress rippling in the breeze—stepped out from behind a headstone. Then she returned to her burial crypt, where she climbed into her coffin and closed the lid. Lucy—now a vampire created by Count Dracula—had satisfied her need to drink human blood for another night.

The next morning at the Seward Sanitarium, Martin, Renfield's attendant, read the local newspaper as he sipped his morning tea. THE WHITBY HORROR CONTINUES! the large headline proclaimed.

"Listen to this," Martin said to a nurse sitting near him. He read from the paper: "'Further attacks on small children, committed after dark by the mysterious woman in white, took place last night. Every child attacked described a beautiful woman in a white dress who promised them candy. The children were then lured to a secluded spot and bitten in the neck.'"

Martin put down the paper. "What do you think of that?" he asked the nurse.

"Ghosts?" she guessed.

Martin shook his head. "Vampires!" he said knowingly. "Vampires!"

Early that evening, just before sunset, Mina was sitting on the sanitarium's terrace with Jonathan Harker and Professor Van Helsing. Harker, visibly upset, held a newspaper whose headlines blared out the terrible story of the woman in white. The three of them had been discussing Lucy Weston.

"About Miss Lucy and this woman in white," Van Helsing said to Mina, continuing their conversation in an even tone.

"How could Lucy possibly know anything about the woman in white?" asked Harker, exasperated.

"Please, Mr. Harker," said the professor wearily. "Allow me to continue."

He turned back to Mina. "You told me earlier that you saw Lucy Weston after she was buried?"

"Yes, that's right," answered Mina nervously. "I

was here on the terrace one night, and Lucy came out of the shadows, out there on the lawn. She was dressed in a beautiful white dress. She stood looking at me. I started to speak to her, then I remembered . . ." She paused, starting to cry. "I remembered she was dead! The most horrible expression came over Lucy's face—like a hungry animal, a wolf! Then she turned and ran off into the darkness."

Van Helsing leaned toward Mina. "Then you already know that the woman in white is—"

"Lucy!" cried Mina. "Yes, I know. Lucy is the woman in white!"

Van Helsing looked down into Mina's troubled eyes. "Miss Mina," he said comfortingly, "Lucy will remain at rest soon. I promise you that. Her soul will be released from this endless horror."

Mina stood up. "If you can save Lucy's soul after death," she pleaded, "then promise you'll save mine, too!"

Harker rushed to her side. "But you're not going to die, my darling!" he exclaimed. "You're going to go on living!" He started to put his arms around her.

"No, John!" she cried, pushing him away. "You must never touch me again!"

"What are you saying?" asked Harker, totally devastated.

Mina turned to Van Helsing. "Oh, you tell him,

Professor," she pleaded. "Make him understand. I can't!"

Van Helsing looked at her helplessly. He had been trying to explain this whole matter to Harker for days, but the stubborn fool refused to believe him.

Mina turned to Harker. "John," she began, speaking tenderly, "it's all over. Our love, our life together. I love you, John, but this horror has changed me. He commands me and I must obey!" She sank down in her seat and began to cry again.

Van Helsing looked up at the setting sun. "Miss Mina," he said forcefully, "you must come indoors."

Harker was furious. "Professor!" he shouted. "Do you know what you're doing to her? You're driving her crazy! And you're driving her away from me!"

"Mr. Harker," the professor said calmly, pointing at the orange sky, "that is what you should be worrying about. The last rays of the day's sun are disappearing. Soon another night will be upon us."

Harker, not wanting to hear anything else, turned and stormed through the double french doors that led into the library. Van Helsing and Mina followed him.

Dr. Seward was in the library, catching up on some work.

"Dr. Seward," Harker said angrily, "I've had enough of all this vampire nonsense. I'm taking Mina to London with me tonight!"

"But, John . . ." protested Seward.

Harker, ignoring him, turned to Mina. "Mina, please get your bags packed! We're going to London."

"Seward," Van Helsing shouted, appealing to the doctor's authority, "I must be in charge of this situation or I can do nothing for Miss Mina!"

At that moment a nurse entered the library. "Miss Mina's bedroom has been prepared with wolfsbane, as you ordered, Professor," she said.

"Very good, Nurse Briggs," Van Helsing replied. He turned to Mina. "Now you will be safe, Miss Mina, if Dracula returns."

"She's going to be safe," said Harker, "because she's leaving with me for London at once!"

"No, John, please," pleaded Mina. She turned to Dr. Seward. "Father, talk to him!"

Van Helsing, ignoring this exchange, spoke to Nurse Briggs: "Miss Mina is to wear a wreath of wolfsbane when she goes to bed. Watch her closely and see that she does not remove it in her sleep."

"I understand, Professor," replied the nurse.

"And, Nurse Briggs, under no circumstances must her bedroom window be opened tonight," added Van Helsing.

Harker, seeing that Van Helsing had clearly taken charge, pressed Dr. Seward for help. "Well, Doctor," he asked, "are you going to listen to him or to me?"

"John, be patient," replied Seward. "I know you love her, but she's my daughter and I must do what I think is best. Mina, you should go to your room and put on the wolfsbane as the professor suggests."

Mina nodded and left the library, accompanied by Nurse Briggs. When she was gone, Seward turned to Harker.

"John," he began, "I trust Professor Van Helsing. I think we should follow his advice."

"But why?" protested Harker. "What proof does he have?"

"Mr. Harker," began Van Helsing, "I have devoted my entire life to the study of vampires. I know things—unnatural things—that, perhaps, the world is better off not knowing.

"The family name Dracula has been connected with vampire legends in Central Europe for hundreds of years. I was suspicious when I first heard that a Dracula was living near the sanitarium. When I saw that our count cast no reflection in the mirror, I was sure he was one of the undead. I then investigated the ship that carried him here from England, and found that a box of Transylvanian earth had been delivered for him to Carfax Abbey.

"Knowing that vampires must sleep in their native soil by day, I take this as proof that Count Dracula is the vampire terrorizing England."

"I just want to get Mina away from this horror," replied Harker, who, for the first time, was beginning to believe Van Helsing.

"In order to save Miss Mina," the professor explained, "we must find the resting place of Dracula's living corpse and drive a wooden stake through his heart!"

Suddenly Renfield, who had been in the hallway secretly listening to this conversation, stepped into the library.

"Renfield!" snapped Seward.

"What does your master want from you now?" asked Van Helsing.

"My master?" said Renfield. "I have no master. I—" He stopped short, a look of fear coming over his face.

"Dracula must be near," announced Van Helsing. "I can see it in Renfield's expression." He glanced at the doors leading to the terrace.

Dracula was standing outside.

"There he is!" shouted the professor, pointing to the double french doors. The others looked over to the doors, but there was no one to be seen. Dracula had ducked out of sight.

"Get Renfield back into his room," ordered Van Helsing. "Dracula is here, but I must face him by myself."

Dr. Seward and Harker led Renfield out of the library, leaving Van Helsing alone in the room.

"I am here, Count Dracula!" shouted Van Helsing. "And this time I am ready for you!"

CHAPTER 9
Confrontation

Dracula stepped into the library from the terrace.

"Van Helsing," he said in a commanding tone. The professor turned to face the evil Count.

"Now that you have discovered the truth," Dracula continued, "it would be wise for you to return to your own country!"

"I shall remain here," the professor said evenly. "I must protect those whom you would destroy!"

"You are too late," said the vampire, smiling triumphantly. "My blood now flows through Mina's veins. She will live through the centuries to come, as I have lived!"

"We know how to save Miss Mina's soul, if not her life," Van Helsing stated.

"Ah, yes, the stake," said Dracula, sneering. "But

you see, Professor, you do not know all there is to know about vampires. The staking of my heart will free her soul only if she dies by day. I shall see to it that she dies by night!"

"And I shall see to it that Carfax Abbey is torn down, stone by stone!" Van Helsing shouted, his rage growing. He pointed a threatening finger at the Count. "I will find your hiding place. Then, in the bright glare of the sunlight you so dread, I will rip the cover from your coffin and drive that stake through your heart. And I will do this while Miss Mina still lives!"

A disturbed look came over Dracula's face, and he clutched his chest. A moment later, however, he regained his composure. "Many have tried to stop me in the past five hundred years," he said, his burning red eyes staring intently at Van Helsing. "All have died—and the deaths were often very unpleasant."

Van Helsing stiffened his body, bracing himself against the vampire's piercing stare.

"Come here," Dracula commanded, slowly raising his hand. "Come here, Professor Van Helsing!"

Van Helsing used all of his willpower to resist the powerful command. Then Dracula exerted even more pressure on Van Helsing's mind. Still the professor did not budge.

"Your will is strong, Van Helsing," said Dracula.

Van Helsing reached into his jacket pocket.

"More wolfsbane, Professor?" asked the vampire, sounding amused.

"Something more effective than wolfsbane, Count," Van Helsing taunted.

Dracula, unwilling to play this game any longer, bared his fangs and opened his cape, then moved in for the kill.

Van Helsing pulled out a large silver cross, which he held out toward the vampire.

Dracula turned in horror, covering his face with his cape. Then, hissing and snarling, he fled from the house, racing off into the night.

Harker, in the meantime, had decided to visit Mina and check on her condition. As he approached the door to her room, he could hear the girl inside speaking to Nurse Briggs.

"Open the window, Briggs," Mina begged. She was sitting up in bed, looking rested and alert. "I need some air. The odor from that horrible wolfsbane is stifling!"

"We mustn't open the window!" Nurse Briggs exclaimed. "The professor—"

"Oh, never mind the professor!" Mina cried, rising swiftly from her bed.

"Go back to bed at once," ordered Briggs. "If you

don't, I'm going to have to call your father! Please, do what I say!"

Mina ignored the nurse and walked out of her bedroom onto the balcony.

Briggs ran from the room to seek help, then saw Harker, who had been waiting in the hallway.

"Miss Mina—" cried the nurse.

"What's wrong?" asked Harker, concerned.

"She's out on the balcony," Briggs explained. "She refuses to obey Professor Van Helsing's orders."

"Let me see her!" shouted Harker.

Mina, hearing his voice, came running out into the hallway.

"Oh, John, I'm so glad you're here," she said, rushing into his arms. "They've kept me locked in my room with that horrible-smelling wolfsbane. It's been like a nightmare. I—John, why are you looking at me like that?"

"Mina!" he cried, gazing warmly into her bright eyes. "You look so much better! You're like a changed woman."

"Why, yes, I—I feel wonderful," she said, realizing it was true. "I've never felt better in my life!"

"I've been so worried about you," said her fiancé, taking her hand.

"Excuse me, Mr. Harker," interrupted Nurse Briggs. "I think Miss Mina should go to sleep now."

"That's all right, Briggs," said Harker. "I'll keep an eye on her."

"Run along, Briggs," added Mina. "And don't worry so much!"

"Well, all right," said Briggs reluctantly, going downstairs.

As soon as they were alone, Mina and Harker walked through the bedroom and out onto the balcony.

"Look, John, the fog is lifting," said Mina, pointing up to the night sky. "See how plainly you can see the stars?"

"Yes," replied Harker. "I can see millions of them."

As Harker scanned the night sky, his head bent back. Mina stared at his exposed throat. Her lips pulled back slightly to reveal two small fangs that had begun to grow in her mouth. Her eyes vacant, she moved her head toward Harker's neck.

"I've never seen the stars so close," said Harker, still looking up. "I feel that I could reach out and touch them." He looked at Mina and noticed her strange expression. "Mina, what's wrong?" he cried, alarmed.

Startled by Harker's shocked tone, the girl came out of her trance.

"Nothing's wrong, John," she replied calmly, her

expression returning to normal. "Everything's fine. Come, let's sit down."

Mina sat on the chaise longue, gently pulling Harker down next to her.

Professor Van Helsing rushed into Dr. Seward's private study.

"Professor, what is it?" asked Seward, looking up from his papers.

"I have spoken with Dracula!" cried Van Helsing urgently. "That which I have feared from the beginning has come to pass! Dracula has fused his blood with Miss Mina's. Unless we do something soon, she will die!"

"But, Professor, I—"

"Don't argue with me!" said Van Helsing sternly. "There's not a moment to lose! If Mina dies, she will become a vampire like Dracula. Come, follow me!"

The two of them quickly left the study and hurried upstairs to Mina's bedroom.

Alone on the balcony, Mina and Harker sat quietly under the stars. Then, as the fog started to roll back in, Mina grew lively.

"I love the fog, John," she said. "I love the fog and the night."

"But only yesterday you said you were afraid of

the night," responded Harker, puzzled by yet another change in his fiancée's mood.

"I could never have said anything so silly," she said, laughing. "After all, what is there to be afraid of? The night is the only time I feel alive!"

Suddenly a bat flew onto the balcony and hovered in midair. Mina stood up, then walked toward it.

"Be careful, Mina," warned Harker, springing up and running after her. "That bat will get tangled in your hair."

But Mina stood perfectly still, her eyes vacant. "I will," she said woodenly, responding to a voice only she could hear. "I will."

Just as suddenly as it had appeared, the bat flew away.

"You will what?" Harker asked, confused by Mina's strange words.

Mina snapped out of her trance. "I didn't say anything!"

"Yes, you did," said Harker. "You said, 'I will.'"

Mina held out her hand. "John, come sit with me."

At that same moment, Dr. Seward and Van Helsing came down the hallway to Mina's bedroom and knocked at the door. When no one answered, they entered and saw the empty bed.

"She's gone!" cried the professor.

"How can we save her?" asked Seward.

"There's only one way," replied Van Helsing. "Dracula must be destroyed!"

Just then they heard Mina's voice on the balcony.

Mina held Harker's hand and spoke softly and tenderly. But as she talked, she was following a command she did not remember receiving.

"John," she said, "that silly old professor has a big silver cross. I want you to get it away from him and hide it."

"But why?" asked Harker.

"Oh, you know what he's like," she replied. "He'll be wanting to protect me again. From the night or Count Dracula or some such nonsense. There's no need for that."

"But I'm beginning to think the professor is right," said Harker. "He's told me some terrible things about Count Dracula."

Mina let out a strange, unnatural laugh.

"Why do you laugh?" asked her fiancé uneasily.

She stared at him, an eerie reddish glow in her eyes.

"Why do you look at me that way? Your eyes!"

Mina, saying nothing, moved her face toward Harker's, her lips drawing back as her fangs began to descend on Harker's throat.

"Mina!" he cried. "Mina, what are you doing?"

Dr. Seward rushed out onto the balcony, followed by Van Helsing, who was holding his silver cross out in front of him. At the sight of the cross, Mina shrank back in terror, covering her eyes and snarling.

"What are you trying to do, Van Helsing?" shouted Harker. "Frighten her to death?"

"No!" said Van Helsing. "I'm trying to save her!"

"John!" cried Mina, still shielding her eyes. "Make him put the cross away. I can't stand to look at it!"

"But why?" asked Harker.

Mina looked up at him, tears in her eyes. "I can't tell you," she replied.

"You must," cried Harker. "I have a right to know. We all do!"

Mina broke down and began crying. "Everything Van Helsing has said is the truth," she sobbed. "Dracula has come to me. He opened a vein in his arm and made me drink his blood! And now he can control me!" As soon as she finished speaking, Mina collapsed in a faint.

Harker rushed to her side. Gently lifting her up, he carried her back into her bedroom.

CHAPTER 10
Crypt of the Undead

The next night Mina once again slept restlessly. There was wolfsbane hanging throughout her room, and the window was locked. Nurse Briggs sat in a chair by her side, reading.

After several hours Briggs grew sleepy. She stood up and walked to the window. She stared outside for a few moments, trying to clear her drowsy head.

Count Dracula stood on the lawn below, looking up at Mina's window. He had been there for hours, waiting for an opportunity like this one. When he spotted Nurse Briggs looking out, he turned all his power toward her.

As soon as their eyes met, he silently commanded Briggs to remove the wolfsbane from the room. She obeyed. Then he told her to unlock and open the window. Again she followed his command.

Dracula transformed himself into a bat and flew into Mina's bedroom. When he had changed back into his human form, he commanded Nurse Briggs to leave the room.

Alone with Mina now, he moved to her bedside and leaned over her sleeping form. He buried his fangs in her neck and drank her blood. Then he roused her and led her away from the house. Mina walked by his side in a trance, her eyes staring blankly ahead as they crossed the sanitarium's lawn, heading for Dracula's home in neighboring Carfax Abbey.

Hidden in the shadows of Carfax Abbey were Professor Van Helsing and Jonathan Harker. They were lying in wait for Dracula. The professor knew that if he didn't stop Dracula now, it would be too late to save Mina, for she could not last another night. Harker, believing Mina to be safe in the care of Nurse Briggs, had left her side and agreed to help the professor put an end to this terrible reign of death and horror. They planned to follow Dracula to his resting place and wait for the morning sun. Then they would kill him.

Suddenly they spotted someone moving across the abbey's grounds.

"It's Renfield," whispered Harker. "He's gotten out again. He must be on his way to see his master."

"Let's go, Harker," said Van Helsing excitedly. "He might show us a way into Dracula's crypt!" They followed Renfield around to the side of the abbey.

Renfield pushed his way through the surrounding brush to a small iron door, concealed by high weeds. He fumbled with the latch for a few seconds, then opened the door and slipped inside.

He reached the bottom of a long, curving set of stone steps. Then, far above, he heard Count Dracula and Mina entering the abbey through another door.

"Master!" Renfield shouted. "I'm here!" He ran up the stairs toward Dracula and Mina. "What is it, master? What do you want me to do?"

Meanwhile, outside, Harker and Van Helsing were searching the abbey's wall, not knowing how Renfield had gotten inside. "There's got to be a door here someplace," said Van Helsing, frantically pushing aside the thick weeds.

"Look, Professor!" shouted Harker. "An opening in the wall!" He had found a gap in the abbey's lower wall where one of the ancient stones was missing. Peering in, he gasped in shock as he saw Dracula, Mina, and Renfield.

"Mina!" shouted Harker. "Mina! I'm here!"

Dracula turned at the sound of his voice and saw Harker's face through the hole in the wall. His own face livid, he turned accusing eyes on Renfield.

"I didn't lead them here, master!" said Renfield, backing down the stairs away from Dracula. "I swear, master! I didn't know they were following me!"

The vampire started down the stairs toward Renfield, moving slowly and deliberately. The air was thick with impending doom.

Renfield backed away quickly, but Dracula raised his hand and issued a command: "Wait!"

Renfield froze in his tracks. "Master, I've been loyal," he cried. "I've been your slave. I didn't betray you!"

Dracula continued moving down the stairs.

"Master, don't kill me," pleaded his creature. "Punish me, torture me, but let me live."

Dracula grabbed Renfield by the neck and lifted him off his feet, ignoring the frantic pleas and tightening his powerful grasp until Renfield stopped struggling. Dracula tossed his limp body down the stairs. The miserable wretch lay in a lifeless heap on the stone floor.

Harker and Van Helsing witnessed this gruesome execution through the opening in the wall. Urgently, they resumed their search for the door.

"I found it!" Harker called a few minutes later, pushing aside the tall weeds and flinging open the iron door.

As the two men burst inside, Dracula—Mina

draped across his arms—was approaching a heavy wooden door that led to the burial crypt.

"Mina! We're coming!" shouted Harker as he and Van Helsing ran toward them.

Dracula, using his supernatural powers, opened the door to the crypt without touching it. Then, carrying Mina, he slipped through. The huge door slammed behind him just as Van Helsing and Harker reached it.

"We've got to get in before it's too late!" cried Van Helsing.

Harker, struggling to open the massive door, cried, "He'll kill her if we don't stop him!"

Just then the first faint rays of the morning sun came creeping in through the open iron door, shining almost imperceptibly on the wooden door to the crypt.

Van Helsing noticed it first. "Day is breaking!" he shouted triumphantly. "We have him trapped. I only hope we aren't too late to save Miss Mina!"

Both men put their shoulders to the door, jarring it open slightly.

Beyond the wooden door, deep in the tunnels of the crypt, Dracula growled ferociously and pressed on toward his coffin, hurrying away from the sunlight that was beginning to stream into the crypt through a crack in the wall.

Harker and Van Helsing found an old piece of timber to use as a battering ram. With a running start, they smashed into the huge door. It flew open. Inside they heard a bloodcurdling scream.

"That was Mina!" shouted Harker, frozen with fear. Van Helsing ran on ahead. "Mina! Where are you?" Harker cried. But now there was no response.

"Harker, I've found them!" called Van Helsing from one of the crypt's rooms. Harker, running to join him, found the professor standing next to two identical coffins.

"Where's Mina?" asked Harker desperately.

Van Helsing pointed to the two closed coffins. "I'm sorry, Harker," said the professor compassionately. "It appears we are too late to save her."

Harker fell back against a wall, overwhelmed by grief.

"You must be strong," said Van Helsing forcefully. "You must help me destroy Dracula so that at least we can save Miss Mina's soul. Get me something I can use as a hammer."

Quivering with shock, Harker stumbled off.

Van Helsing, meanwhile, found an old board and smashed it against the stone wall. The wood splintered into many pieces. Then he took the longest piece, which had a sharp point, and walked over to one of the coffins. He lifted the lid.

Dracula lay inside, asleep.

Harker had returned with a heavy flat metal hinge. He handed it to Van Helsing and looked away as the professor placed the sharp point of the makeshift stake on top of Dracula's chest. Then, summoning all his strength, Van Helsing brought the heavy hinge down, driving the splinter deep into the vampire's heart.

Dracula howled and hissed, his body twitching and shuddering. Then he let out a final groan and fell silent. The vampire was dead—this time forever.

Harker, standing beside Van Helsing, grasped the lid of the second coffin and braced himself. He expected to see his beloved Mina lying in this awful box. They flung open the lid.

The coffin was empty.

"She's not here!" exclaimed Van Helsing.

"Then she may be alive!" cried Harker hopefully.

"John! John, I'm here!" came Mina's familiar voice. Harker, followed by Van Helsing, dashed down a tunnel and turned a corner. There was Mina, very much alive. She and Harker embraced, relief flooding through both of them.

"I heard you calling, John," said Mina. "But I couldn't answer. I was still under his control."

"When Dracula died, you were released from his power," explained Van Helsing.

"We thought he'd killed you," said Harker, overwhelmed with joy.

"The daylight stopped him," Mina told them. "When he saw the sunlight, he dropped me and ran for his coffin."

"There is nothing more to fear, Miss Mina," said Van Helsing. "Dracula is dead. And when he died, so did those he made into vampires. That means Miss Lucy can finally rest in peace. But come, let us leave this place of death."

Van Helsing, Harker, and Mina made their way back through the crypt, out the wooden door, and up the long stone stairs. Then they left the abbey and stepped out into the bright morning sun.